ACO Jess & Friends

RACCOON RESCUE

Dedicated to:

Owen, Lily, Quinn, Avery, and Nicole

Love, Aunt Jessie

Copyright 2021 ACO Jess & Friends LLC, Philadelphia, PA

Printed in China

Limited 1st Edition

ISBN: 978-1-7378539-0-9

www.acojessandfriends.com

ACO Jess & Friends

RACCOON RESCUE

Written by Jessica Thedinga   Illustrated by Deborah Tyson

Meet Jess, she is an Animal Control Officer who helps animals every day for work. These are her pets, Freddy and Frankie the dogs, and a cat named Nefertiti.

Before work she feeds her pets,

walks the dogs,

kisses them goodbye,

and tells the dogs their friend will come walk them soon.

In her van the radio yelled.

ACO Jess, a raccoon needs your help at 315 Shady Lane

I'm on my way!

The raccoon, unsure of Jess, growled.

"Don't worry little buddy I will get you out."

ACO Jess tipped the can over and the raccoon raced off.

"Wait, why aren't you going to take it away? It's probably sick, it's out in the daytime!" yelled the woman.

"We do not take away animals. We help them. Raccoons do not have a bedtime. It is normal to see them in the daytime too, especially if you threw away yummy food."

"Oh, if it is not sick I guess it was kind of cute. Thank you," replied the woman.

"Hello, I am here to help with the..."

The child interrupted shouting, "They are upstairs!"

The raccoons had fallen from a hole in the ceiling.

"How did you get inside?" Jess knew the raccoons would not answer, but hoped her calm voice would make them feel safe.

Jess put a cage close to the raccoons. To her surprise, the smaller one walked right in. **"Well you made that easy! I will go get your buddy and bring you outside."**

The other raccoon ran into a bedroom to hide and got stuck in a fold up bed.

Jess walked closer to the raccoon with her control stick, **"I am not going to hurt you. This tool helps me safely pick you up so I can take you outside."**

In the woods near the house, Jess opened the cages and shouted, **"You are free!"** as the raccoons ran off.

People in the city gathered to see the raccoons. They asked Jess so many questions. She loves to talk to people and teach them about animals and her job as an animal control officer.

She pulled into the park and saw a raccoon with a soup can on its head! Jess parked the van, jumped out, and ran over to the animal.

"I am just going to pull gently. It is going to be alright, pumpkin."

She pulled a few times, but it did not work.

One more big tug and the can came right off!

Jess looked around and saw trash scattered all over the park, even up in a bird's nest.

"When you litter you can hurt animals and it is terrible for our Earth!"

She started to clean the park so no other animals get hurt. The raccoon picked up a bottle and put it in her bag. **"Aww! Are you trying to help me clean up? Thank you!"**

She put all the trash in her van.

At the house the family told Jess the raccoons fell
through the basement window.

"Come on little ones, let's get you back in the yard so your mom can find you."

"Shouldn't you take them somewhere?" The man asked.

"The best place for a baby wild animal is with its mother."

"There she is!"

They watched the mother raccoon take the babies into the woods.

"Do you think they have rabies? I always heard raccoons were sick if you see them during the day." asked the woman.

"I hear that ALL the time, it's an old myth that raccoons are only awake at night. It's normal to see them out in the day, too, especially in the spring when they have babies to care for."

At the end of a long day of rescuing raccoons, Jess returned home to her pets. She greeted them with hugs and kisses.

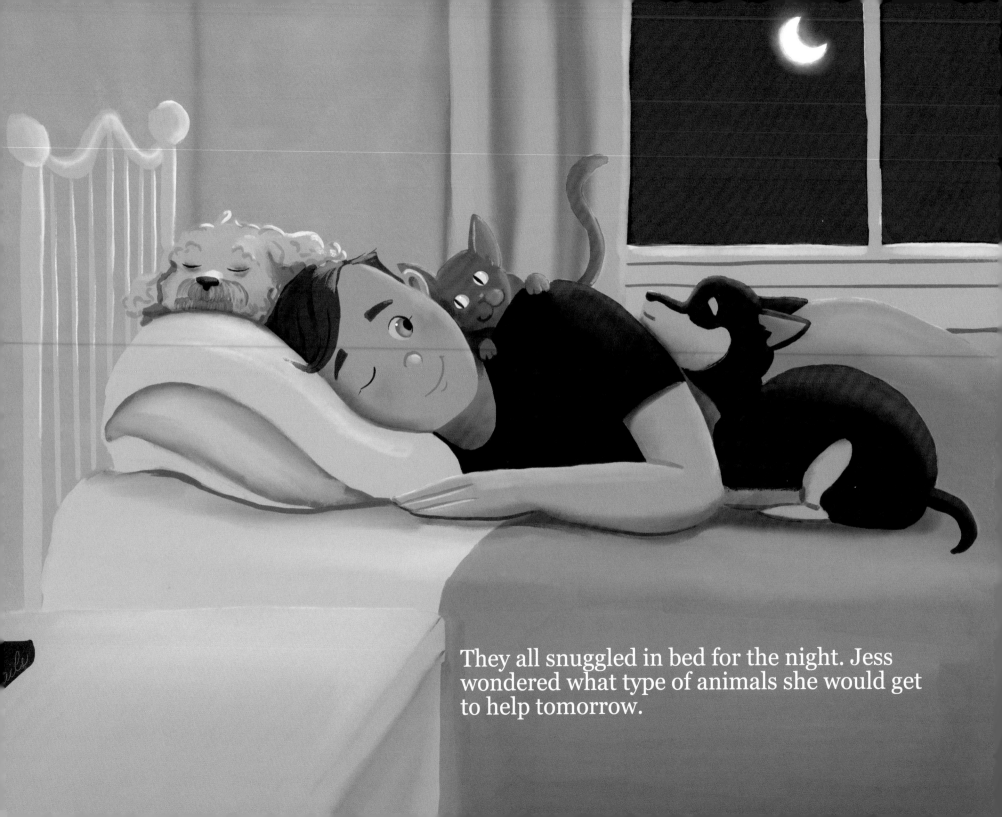

They all snuggled in bed for the night. Jess wondered what type of animals she would get to help tomorrow.

Raccoons can have rabies, but they don't all have it. Being active during the day does NOT mean a wild animal is sick.

HERE ARE SOME SIGNS OF A SICK RACCOON:

Extreme aggression, chasing you

Walking in circles, confused, eyes bouncing back and forth

Stumbling, falling down, or just lying on its side

Mouth foaming, looks wet and messy when it's not raining

Even though they are cute, you should **NEVER** touch a wild animal.

A special "thank you" to everyone who backed my
Kickstarter campaign!

COMING SOON: